D

LIBERTY PORTER
First Daughter

★ ★ ★ JULIA DeVILLERS ★ ★ ★
★ ILLUSTRATED BY PAIGE POOLER ★

LIBERTY PORTER
First Daughter

ALADDIN
NEW YORK   LONDON   TORONTO   SYDNEY

ALADDIN

An imprint of Simon & Schuster Children's Publishing Division
1230 Avenue of the Americas, New York, NY 10020

Text copyright © 2009 by Julia DeVillers

Illustrations copyright © 2009 by Paige Pooler

For information about special discounts for bulk purchases,
please contact Simon & Schuster Special Sales at 1-866-506-1949 or business@simonandschuster.com.

The Simon & Schuster Speakers Bureau can bring authors to your live event.
For more information or to book an event contact the Simon & Schuster Speakers Bureau at 1-866-248-3049
or visit our website at www.simonspeakers.com.

Designed by Karin Paprocki

The text of this book was set in Bauer Bodoni Roman.

The illustrations for this book were rendered digitally.

Manufactured in the United States of America

The Library of Congress has cataloged the hardcover edition as follows:

DeVillers, Julia.

Liberty Porter, first daughter / by Julia DeVillers ; illustrated by Paige Pooler. — 1st Aladdin hardcover ed.

p. cm.

Summary: On her first day at the White House, nine-year-old Liberty exuberantly explores her new home
while making new friends and giving unique tours of her own.

[1. Presidents—Family—Fiction. 2. White House (Washington, D.C.)—Fiction.

3. Family life—Washington, D.C.—Fiction. 4. Washington (D.C.)—Fiction.

5. Friendship—Fiction.] I. Pooler, Paige, ill. II. Title.

PZ7.D4974Li 2009 / [Fic]—dc22 / 2009008916

ISBN 978-1-4169-9711-5 / ISBN 978-1-4169-9571-5 (eBook)

To the children of America

LIBERTY PORTER
First Daughter

Chapter 1

IF YOUR FATHER IS ABOUT TO BECOME PRESIDENT of the United States, there are a few things you might want to know.

1. Inauguration Day is the day a new president starts the job.

2. Riding in the backward seat of the limo to Inauguration Day seems really cool. But it actually can make you kind of sick to your stomach.

3. And then if you ask your dad to switch seats because you are feeling sick, don't forget that you put something on the seat next to you: a congratulations card that you decorated in glitter glue. And maybe the glitter glue hadn't exactly dried yet. And your dad sits on it.

Liberty was learning all this new and important information today! Inauguration Day!! It was a historical day for America. And also a historical day for Liberty Porter.

Because Liberty Porter's father was the guy who was going to be president!

This meant that LIBERTY PORTER WAS ABOUT TO BE FIRST DAUGHTER!

Liberty had been nonstop excited since the election. But she needed to be serious now for just a moment.

★ ★ 2 ★ ★

Liberty had watched out the windows at they'd driven through Washington, D.C. And now the limo had pulled up to the Capitol, the building where the country's laws are made.

Her mother smiled at her as she slid out of the limo. And then her father was getting up too.

"Um, Dad?" Liberty said. "Before you get out, I have two things I have to tell you."

"Of course, honey," her dad said.

"The first thing is that I made you a card!" Liberty said. "The second thing is that it's stuck to your, um, butt."

Her father turned around and looked surprised. He peeled the card off his pants and held it up. Whew! The glitter smiley faces had smudged, but the rest of the card still looked good.

"Well, thank you," he said. "What a surprise. You usually just hand me the cards you make."

★ ★ 3 ★ ★

"Read it!" Liberty said.

Her father read out loud:

You're PRES-TASTIC! You're PRES-TACULAR!

You're PRESIDENT!!!!

Love your First (and Only!) Daughter,

Liberty Porter

☺ ☺ ☺

"I love it," her father said. "I'll hang it up in my new office."

The Oval Office!!

"And what was the second thing you wanted to tell me?" he asked her.

"The glitter glue wasn't dry," Liberty told him.

Um, yeah. There were very sparkly faces smiling from the back of his pants.

The next few minutes were kind of busy. Liberty's

family had to Hurry! Because it was almost time for the Big Ceremony!

But the new president couldn't exactly go with sparkly smiley faces on him. So first there was this whole "Oh, no! What gets glitter glue off of a suit?" situation. The bad news was: You can't. The good news was, the suit jacket was long enough to cover it, mostly.

"Well, now I'm happy on the inside and outside," her father said. Liberty's father smiled at her, and she knew everything was totally fine. Everyone always said Liberty and her dad shared the same smile, black hair, and laugh.

So finally they were ready. Liberty followed her parents up the ginormous steps of the Capitol building. This was where a new president took the oath of office.

Liberty's dad had told her a couple days ago that the oath of office was a promise. He would raise his right hand. And in front of millions of people, he would say a promise to do his best as president.

There had been fewer than fifty people ever who had been president of the United States. It started with George Washington. And today it would continue with William Porter.

Liberty had put that fact in the research report she'd written the month before at her old school. It was about all the presidents and their families. She'd called it "What Happened Before the Porters Took Over the White House."

Liberty had gotten an A+ on it! A+ = Awesomely Perfect! She did not always get an A+ Awesomely Perfect on her schoolwork.

Liberty suddenly felt nervous. What if she was not an A+ First Daughter? What if she was really bad at being a First Daughter?

Liberty's stomach suddenly felt sickish again.

"It's almost time, sweetie," her mom said to her.

Liberty looked up at her mother. She looked very happy, but a little frozen. There were snowflakes melting on her mom's medium-length brown hair. Her mom's cheeks were almost as red as her deep red coat.

Liberty shivered. She didn't know if it was from the cold or from her nervous feeling.

"Mom," Liberty said. "I'm not one hundred percent positive I know how to be a First Daughter."

"I think that's okay, sweetie." Her mom smiled. "You'll learn as you go. And to be honest, I'm not one hundred percent positive I know how to be a first lady. I've never been one before, you know."

★ ★ 7 ★ ★

"Well, at least I know I won't do what President Theodore Roosevelt's son did," Liberty said. "He dropped a giant snowball off the roof of the White House onto a policeman's head!"

"Then you're off to a good start," her mother said.

"And I'm not going to bring a pony into the White House elevator like he did either," Liberty said.

"And I appreciate that," her mother said.

"But some First Kids had ponies and they never brought them inside! President John Kennedy's daughter had a pony named Macaroni."

"Yes, I know." Liberty's mom smiled. "And I think I know where this conversation is heading."

"Oh," Liberty said. "Then I'll just skip straight to the part where I ask really nicely: May I pretty please have a pony?"

"Sorry, but no," her mother said.

Well, it was worth a try.

"However, you *may* take Franklin in the elevator," her mom said. "He'll like that."

Liberty's dog, Franklin, *would* like that! Thinking about her dog made Liberty feel much happier. Her mom reached over and gave her a big hug. Liberty suddenly felt the sickishness leave her stomach. Not all of it. But most.

"Daddy doesn't really know how to be president yet either," Liberty pointed out. "I think we're all going to have to wing it."

"Sounds like a plan," her mom said.

"It's almost time!" someone whispered. "Places!"

Liberty's father came over and stood next to her. Liberty's father was about to become president of the United States of America. For real.

Her father leaned down and looked her right in the

eye. "My Liberty is about to become First Daughter," he said to her. "You will represent the children of America. The future of our country."

Liberty's father raised his right hand, like he was going to take an oath. He waited.

Oh! Liberty had to take an oath too! She didn't know that part! Okay! She took a deep breath and raised her right hand too.

"I, Liberty Porter, promise to be an awesome First Daughter. I will represent the children of America, who are the future of our country!" Liberty promised.

Suddenly, Liberty knew she would. The oath made her feel official. It made her feel ready!

Then Liberty's father let out a laugh.

"What?" Liberty said. "Did I oath my office wrong?"

"I was just raising my hand to give you a high five." Her dad smiled. "You didn't have to take an oath."

Oh. That was kind of embarrassing. Her father raised his hand again. Liberty gave him a high five.

"You don't have to be so serious. I don't want you to worry about a thing. Your job is to just be a nine-year-old," her father said.

"But I *want* to be serious," Liberty said.

Liberty knew he said that to make her not feel pressure. But hello? She could be *very* helpful! All nine-year-olds knew that they were capable of big things. *Very* big things.

She wanted to oath her office! She wanted to tell her father she could help! She could be his assistant! But she didn't have the chance.

Because suddenly and loudly, a voice boomed over the microphone.

"Ladies and gentlemen, please stand for the oath of office."

Okay! Okay! The real oath of office!

★ ★ 11 ★ ★

Liberty's mom took Liberty's hand. Her dad took her other hand. And they walked out onto an area on the steps. Her dad stood in front of an Important Judge. Liberty could see the vice president and her husband. Their kids were there too. But they were grown-ups and not kids anymore.

Liberty was the only real kid up there. And definitely the shortest person. The steps up to the Capitol building were huge. The white dome on top of the Capitol building was huge. And the crowd was huge.

Liberty looked out to see about a gajillion people, waving their I'm a Porter SupPorter! posters.

Hey! And there she was, smiling back! Okay, what also was huge was her huge face smiling back from giant TV screens. Whoa. Whoa and whoa. People all over the world and even back at her old school were watching her face on TV right this very second!

People like Max Mellon. Liberty remembered what

★ ★ 12 ★ ★

Max had said on her last day of school. Her teacher had let each student say a special good-bye to Liberty.

Most people had said they'd miss her. Max had given her advice.

"You'll probably be on TV," he said.

"Yup," Liberty had agreed. That was true. And that was something Liberty was excited about. Very.

"You're smiling now," Max warned. "But you won't be smiling if . . ."

He shook his head.

"If what?" Liberty had asked him.

"If you sneeze," Max said. "My cousin sneezed on live television once. And green sneeze came flying out all over."

Liberty wished she hadn't thought about this now. Now, while she actually was on TV in real life. Suddenly Liberty's nose started to itch. On the giant-screen TVs, Liberty's nose wiggled.

Uh-oh.

Do not sneeze, she thought to herself. Do. Not. Sneeze.

Her dad raised his right hand. Liberty raised her right hand to itch her nose. A giant Liberty itched her nose on the TV screen.

Then the TV screen showed the crowd. And it showed a close-up of a girl sitting on her father's shoulders. The girl was waving a sign.

The sign said: I ♥ LIBERTY PORTER!

Cool! That sign was for her! Liberty looked around in the crowd for the girl and she spotted her. Liberty waved back at the girl. The girl made a surprised face and nearly fell backward off her father's shoulders. Whoops! But the girl's father held her on. And the girl waved her sign even harder.

Liberty felt her sneeze disappear. Because a feeling had overtaken her. She felt:

Historical.

Patriotic. No, more than patriotic. Patriotical.

Liberty suddenly felt a huge grin spread across her face. Her heart felt like it was about to explode in a good way. That was her own dad and mom up there becoming the president and first lady of America.

And suddenly, like a mute button was pressed, everything was silent. A hush fell over the crowd.

Liberty watched as her father smiled at her mother. He smiled at Liberty. Then he raised his right hand.

"I, William David Porter, do solemnly swear that I will faithfully execute the Office of President of the United States, and will to the best of my ability, preserve, protect, and defend the Constitution of the United States."

Yes. Liberty's father would be here for the country. And so would Liberty. Maybe *some* people thought

a nine-year-old couldn't help too much, but Liberty knew better.

Her father had a lot of people who worked for him. But he didn't have anyone who truly understood the kids of America. The future of America. Until now. Liberty could be her father's assistant, even if he didn't know it. His *secret assistant*.

Yup. She liked the sound of that. Secret Assistant to the President. Liberty felt so patriotical, she was ready to burst! And then she did burst.

"U-S-A!" she shouted. Liberty jumped up. She pumped her fist in the air. "U-S-A!"

She turned around and realized the judge was looking at her. The vice president and her family were looking at her.

"Um," Liberty said. The crowd was looking at her. No, staring at her. Was this going to be worse than green sneeze?

And then she saw the girl on her dad's shoulders wave from the crowd.

"U-S-A!" the girl yelled. "U-S-A!"

And then everyone was chanting.

"U-S-A! U-S-A!"

And then it was so loud, her ears almost exploded. "U-S-A! U-S-A! U-S-A!" People were waving and cheering and chanting.

Liberty saw her dad and mom smile. Her father came off his stand. He leaned down to take her hand. And he whispered in her ear: "That's my Liberty. Liberty Porter, First Daughter."

Chapter 2

SO AFTER THE OATH, THE PRESSURE WAS OFF
for Liberty. But the pressure was on for
her father. He had to give his Inauguration
Speech.

Liberty just had to stand there and pretend not
to be freezing cold. She watched her father give the
speech he'd practiced for her. It was a lot less boring
this time, with all the people cheering him on.

"How did I do?" her father asked her after he was
done speeching.

"Prestacular, President Porter!" Liberty said. She

gave him two white-mittened thumbs-ups.

And then she got to ride in a limo with flashing red, white, and blue headlights! And she watched the biggest parade she'd ever seen in her life! People marching in uniforms playing music! People tossing batons, riding giant floats, and riding horses!

Liberty liked her front-row seat. But she was going to ask if maybe next inauguration she could be in the parade. Ooh, maybe she could ride on one of the horses!

This was the most exciting day of her life! Except maybe not this exact minute. The parade was over. Now she was just waiting for . . . she had no clue. It had been an exciting day. But a long day.

Liberty yawned.

"Liberty, did I just see a yawn?" A woman with a short haircut and a crisp red suit came rushing over. Well, as fast as she could rush in black pointy heels.

Liberty knew this woman. She was her father's new chief of staff, Miss Crum. The chief of staff is in charge of a lot of things, including the president's schedule.

"Perhaps you should wait over here, away from the window," Miss Crum said in her bossy voice. "There are photographers out there."

She also seemed to think she was chief of Liberty. Bluh. Liberty moved away from the window.

"Please stay still," Miss Crum said. "And keep your mouth closed."

Liberty stayed still. Liberty had had to stay still during a lot of My Father Is Running for President stuff. She also had had to sit without squirming or complaining.

At first, it had been impossible. Then came her Most Embarrassing Moment.

Liberty had sat through a lot of speeches in one day. Maybe a gajillion.

And that night, she saw herself on the news. She

always got excited to see herself on TV when her dad was running for president. Liberty would feel like a TV star!

But on this Most Embarrassing Moment Day the news showed her squirming. They showed her wiggling. Then they showed her complaining to her mother. And squirming some more.

"Isn't that adorable," the TV person said. "Liberty Porter has to go potty."

Of course, Max Mellon had seen it. And he started calling her "Porter Potty."

So after that, Liberty had gotten very excellent at sitting still.

Liberty had traveled with her parents on the campaign tour. In California, she pretended she was an actress about to win a huge award, with a big smile on her face. In Maine, she pretended she was frozen solid. In Kansas, she couldn't think of anything for Kansas. So she had a sitting still competition against herself.

In Pennsylvania, she pretended she was the Liberty Bell. When it wasn't ringing, of course. Ha-ha! In New York, she pretended she was the Statue of Liberty!

There were a lot of statues in Washington, D.C. She could see one right in front of her. The Washington Monument was pointing to the sky.

Liberty's father came over and smiled at her.

"I see my Liberty is in the spirit of things," he said to her. "Are you enjoying the view?"

He stood next to her and looked out at the Washington Monument too.

"It was built to honor George Washington, of course," her father said. "There are also memorials to honor Abe Lincoln and Thomas Jefferson."

"Maybe they'll build one for you, Daddy!" Liberty said.

"And maybe they'll build one for you." Her father smiled. "I'm sure you will do important things as well."

Ooh! What would a Liberty Porter monument be?

No offense to the Washington Monument, but it was a little boring. It just looked like a tall pencil.

A Liberty Porter monument would so not be boring.

Liberty reached her hands up in the air. She posed as the Liberty Monument. Liberty stood as still as a monument. Her right leg shook a little bit. But mostly she was totally still.

Miss Crum headed over her way. Liberty stood extra still to impress her with stillness.

"Liberty, please remember there are photographers everywhere today," Miss Crum said.

"Okay," Liberty said, barely moving her mouth. There! Look how still she was! Her right leg was practically frozen in midair!

"That was a hint to please stand in a normal position," Miss Crum said.

Oh.

Liberty hated being per- fectly still and *still* not getting it right. Liberty dropped her arms and right leg. She stood as straight and BORing as the Wash- ington Monument.

"Thank you," Miss Crum said. And then she groaned.

Liberty looked up to see her dog running toward her!

"The dog!" Miss Crum moaned.

"My dog!" Liberty said happily at exactly the same time. She turned to Miss Crum. "Jinx! We both said 'dog' at the same time! So you can't speak till you buy me a soda."

Awesome! Miss Crum couldn't speak! And Franklin was here!

"Franklin!!" Liberty said, hugging him. "How does it feel to be First Dog! The First Jack Russell Terrier of America?"

Franklin jumped up and licked Liberty's cheek. He loved it already!

There had been lots of First Dogs in the White House. Liberty had written about them in her A+

paper. Like Theodore Roosevelt's dog! That dog had ripped the pants right off the ambassador of France! And President Lyndon Johnson's dog! He peed right on the leader of Iran!

Franklin would never do anything like that. Okay, it would be kind of funny, though, if he did. Liberty cracked up a little.

Franklin rolled over so Liberty could scritch his belly. Then Liberty noticed a woman running in the room huffing and puffing and holding Franklin's leash. She ran over to Miss Crum and told her something.

"Did you escape?" Liberty asked Franklin. "I'm so happy you found me."

"Liberty!" Miss Crum came over to her. "Oh dear, the dog is getting fur on your coat."

As Liberty picked a teeny-tiny piece of fur off her coat, a tall man wearing a dark suit came up to them.

"This is Secret Service agent Smith," Miss Crum said. "Agent Smith will be here with you for the rest of the day."

The agent had an earpiece in his ear. He was very, very tall. Liberty had to practically lean back to look at him.

"Hello, Liberty," he said.

"Hello, Agent," Liberty said.

"You may call me SAM," he said in a deep voice.

SAM must stand for Secret Agent Man, Liberty thought. Cool!

SAM was wearing a secret agent suit. And very cool dark glasses with silver rims. Liberty could see her reflection in his glasses. Liberty *had* to have a pair of those glasses.

"May I try on your glasses?" Liberty asked sweetly.

SAM took his glasses off and handed them to Liberty. She slid them on.

Oh, yeah.

He was a Secret Service agent to the president.
And Liberty was the Secret Assistant to the President.
So they were both providing SECRET services to the
president.

They would be like partners. They would both do their best to protect and serve.

"Rugged has arrived," he said into his earpiece.

"Who is Rugged?" Liberty asked him.

"Rugged is your dad's code name," he said. "Reader is your mom's code name."

Liberty knew that all presidents and their families got their own code names. Rugged fit her dad. He was strong and tough. Reader definitely fit her mom. She loved books.

And the First Kids got code names too! Turquoise. Energy. Dynamo. Twinkle. Rosebud. Those were some of the First Kids' names before.

So did this mean they had picked out a code name for Liberty, too? Liberty had been waiting a seriously long time for her name. She had a false alarm once. Max Mellon had told her he saw on the news what her code name was going to be.

"Stinky," Max had told her.

As usual, Max Mellon had no idea what he was talking about. She knew her name was not going to be Stinky. What was it?

"Do I have a code name yet?" Liberty asked him. "Like my dad and mom and you do?"

"*My* code name?" SAM asked.

"You know, SAM?" Liberty lowered her voice to a whisper. "Secret Agent Man?"

SAM laughed.

"My name is really SAM," he said. "Short for Samuel."

Oh.

"But I like your idea better," SAM said. "Do you want to know your code name?"

YES! WHAT WAS HER SECRET CODE NAME?

"Liberty, your code name is . . . ," SAM said.

Liberty held her breath. What was it!?!

"Ruffles."

Ruffles? Her code name was Ruffles?

"Ruffles?" Liberty said.

"You know what ruffles are, don't you?" Miss Crum turned around just in time to butt in. "Ruffles are those darling frills on your precious dress."

Miss Crum thought Liberty didn't know what ruffles were. But oh, she knew. Boy, did she. Liberty could be forced to *wear* ruffles. But she had to be *called* Ruffles?!

Ruffles was *not* a secret code name for the Secret Assistant to the President! Ruffles were frilly, darling, and precious. How could she be taken seriously with a name like Ruffles?

Something would have to be done about this. Liberty was happy to see her parents coming toward her. They would help her fix this whole Ruffles thing.

"Well, don't you look official," her mom said to her.

Liberty realized she was still wearing the Secret Service sunglasses.

"She's a pro already." The agent nodded. "She's going to be a big help around here."

Well. That was better. Maybe the whole ruffles thing could wait. Liberty stood up very straight, just like the agent. She put on her best serious expression.

"All she needs is a suit and a walkie-talkie," the agent said.

"Hmm," her dad said. And he pulled out a small box wrapped in blue and white paper. It had a red bow that sparkled. "Perhaps this will be a start."

"Woo-hoo!" Liberty said. She tore off the paper.

A cell phone! HER VERY OWN CELL PHONE!

"Ahhhhh!" Liberty yelled. "I got a cell phone!"

It was her favorite color: blue. It was shiny. It had a little keyboard so she could text. She could text! Liberty had big plans already for this cell phone. Very. Big. Plans. Liberty could stay in immediate touch with everyone important.

"I'm glad you like the phone," her father said.

"Hmm," said the Miss Crum. "Are you sure we approve of children with cell phones? They can get into mischief with them."

Uh-oh. Just like that, her cell phone dreams could be poof! Gone. Even Liberty knew nine years old was pretty young to have a cell phone.

"Maybe you're right," her father said. "Well, I thought it would be a good way for Liberty to stay connected to me."

"It is!" Liberty said. "It is! I promise no mischief!"

"Hmm," Miss Crum said. "Then you should limit texting and calls to you and her mother. And me."

Liberty had no plans to ever text Miss Crum. None. Ever.

"That's what we will do," her father agreed.

Okay, so no texting world leaders or movie stars. At least for now. At least she got to keep her phone.

Ooh! Then Liberty noticed what else her cell phone could do.

"It's got a camera!" Liberty said. Sweet! Liberty took a picture of Franklin. He looked super cute, of course.

"Say cheesy, Daddy!" Liberty commanded. She took a picture of her father. Then she pointed the phone at her father's Secret Service man.

"Mr. Secret Agent Man," she said, "say cheesy!"

The agent didn't say cheesy. But he did give a little smile.

Liberty took his picture. Then Liberty pointed the camera at Miss Crum.

"Say cheesy!" she said.

Miss Crum did not smile. But it didn't matter, because Liberty moved the camera so the chief of staff's head was cut out of the picture, anyway. Liberty checked to make sure. Yes, her head was missing. Heh. Perfect.

Chapter 3

THE BIGGEST CHALLENGE IN LIBERTY'S LIFE
was about to happen. Liberty was moving
to a new house. Not just any house.
The White House. 1600 Pennsylvania Avenue.

LIBERTY PORTER WAS MOVING INTO THE
WHITE HOUSE! She couldn't believe it.

Only three people in the world would be living in
the White House: Liberty. Her mom. Her dad. And one
dog: Franklin.

Liberty couldn't wait.

"Do we get to go into the White House yet?" she asked her father.

"You mean your new home?" He smiled at her.

"The schedule is for you both and Liberty to stay here for a speech," Miss Crum told Liberty's parents.

Another speech! Liberty had sat through days of speeches! Years of speeches! Another parade would be fine. Another concert, sure. But another speech? She was about to move into a new house! She felt like she was going to burst if she had to wait any longer.

"Are things moved in to the house yet?" her father asked Miss Crum.

"Not everything," Miss Crum said. "The staff is unpacking your boxes. Moving furniture. Hanging pictures. Getting the rooms ready."

Liberty understood. There were a lot of rooms in the White House. A LOT. She'd learned that when she did her research report. She knew there were:

- 132 rooms

- 28 fireplaces

- 8 staircases

And if she had to go to the bathroom? There were thirty-five bathrooms!!

Liberty's parents had visited the White House. The former president and his family had taken them all around. But Liberty hadn't seen it yet. The old president and his family had to move out today. And then quickly, people would move her family's stuff in. Her mom had said it would take only a few hours, which was super-fast to move a whole house!

But to Liberty, it seemed like forever.

Suddenly SAM mumbled into his earpiece. Liberty tried to listen in.

It sounded like "Rbbdrrr. Dbbbbr." Liberty needed to learn this Secret Service language.

"Rbbbddr. Dbbrbdr." Liberty held her ear and practiced the language.

Miss Crum gave her a look.

Grrbbdr.

"Ruffles's bedroom is ready," SAM announced.

In that minute Liberty didn't care that he'd just called her Ruffles. She just cared about the bedroom part.

"Then Liberty should see her room," her father said.

Liberty couldn't help it. She let out a big and loud "Yesss!"

Miss Crum frowned.

"I will have to alert Chief Usher Lee," Miss Crum said. "We will see what he says of this change of plans."

She held up her cell phone to make a call. Liberty held her breath.

"Hmm," Miss Crum said. "Chief Usher Lee said he is looking forward to it."

Yesss! Liberty was going to see her new bedroom in the White House! This was major. Important. Huge.

"Have fun, Liberty Bell," her father said, giving her a hug. "Your mother and I will finish what we have to do. And then we'll meet up with you for a homecoming."

"Okay!" Liberty said. She held up her phone. "Text me!"

And then her mother told Miss Crum to walk Liberty to the door to meet the chief usher. Miss Crum did not look pleased. Liberty made plans to ditch her as soon as possible. That would make them both happy.

Liberty skipped along beside SAM. And they reached the front of the White House.

She. Actually. Lived. In. The. WHITE HOUSE!!! Liberty and Franklin started jumping around.

"Goodness," Miss Crum said. "You do have a lot of energy."

Liberty guessed that meant settle down.

"I do hope you appreciate the importance of the White House," Miss Crum said to Liberty. "It is not just a home for you. It is a museum containing precious objects from history. It is an office where people work."

Liberty was prepared.

"It is a symbol of the United States. The White House stands for freedom and hope," Liberty said proudly. "I am honored to live here."

"Oh," Miss Crum said. "Then we can go in now."

SAM winked at her. Liberty winked back.

Liberty was so ready to go in. She was at the steps of her new home. America's Home.

She stood tall and saluted. And then she walked up the stairs.

Liberty thought about what Miss Crum had said about first impressions. She stood as straight as she could. She walked carefully into the entry.

★ ★ 42 ★ ★

"Welcome, Miss Porter," said a man with black hair, wearing a dark suit with a striped tie. Liberty noticed he had the shiniest black shoes she had ever seen. "I am the chief usher. The staff is very pleased to welcome you to your new home."

"Thank you!" Liberty said in her best polite voice. "I look forward to meeting everyone!"

Liberty hoped that was a good first impression. She held out her hand for an official shake. The chief usher shook her hand.

"Chief Usher Lee is in charge of making sure the White House runs smoothly," Miss Crum told her.

"There are ninety-five people who work here," Chief Usher Lee said. "People who cook, who clean, and who fix things."

"I'll try not to make any messes or break anything," Liberty said. "I will walk and not run."

Chief Usher Lee bent down to look at Liberty.

He looked her straight in the eye. "Liberty," he said. "First children have run through these halls for two hundred years. They have walked on stilts and roller-skated. They sat on kitchen trays and slid down the staircases."

"Goodness!" Miss Crum gasped.

"I don't think the kitchen trays are a good idea," Chief Usher agreed. "But you do *not* have to walk slowly."

Liberty looked at the shiny, very clean floor.

"This floor is very shiny," Liberty observed. "And very clean."

"And *very* slippery," Chief Usher Lee said.

Liberty looked at Chief Usher Lee. And he nodded. That was all Liberty needed. Liberty slipped off her shoes. And took a running start and . . .

Woooooosh!

Liberty slid down the hall! She was probably going

three thousand miles per hour! Liberty slid halfway across the room.

"Woo-hoo!" Liberty yelled.

"Liberty!" Miss Crum gasped.

But Chief Usher Lee started clapping.

"Bravo!" Chief Usher Lee called. "And it shall go down in the history books. Liberty Porter entered the White House with a most impressive slide."

Liberty had a feeling she was going to like Chief Usher Lee.

Liberty fixed her tights where they had gotten stuck between her toes. She slid her black shoes back on. She ignored that Miss Crum had her hands over her eyes and was shaking her head.

"Are you ready to see your room now?" Chief Usher Lee asked.

Liberty was ready. Very, very ready.

Chapter 4

THE FLOOR OF THE WHITE HOUSE IS OPEN TO the public," Chief Usher Lee said. "That means people from everywhere can visit. But the second and third floors are only for the president's family and guests."

Woo-hoo!

Liberty had pictured the moment when she would see her new room. She wanted it to be a huge, surprising moment. She covered her eyes with her hands so she couldn't see.

"Okay!" she said, in total darkness. "I'm ready! I won't peek!"

"Is that a good idea?" Miss Crum asked. "You might bump into something valuable. You might fall down the stairs. You might—"

"I'll usher her safely," Chief Usher Lee said. And Liberty could tell it was him who took her arm. He led the way.

"Your room is the East Bedroom," Chief Usher said.

Was the East Bedroom. Now, it would be the Secret Assistant to the President's headquarters, disguised as Liberty's bedroom. Very important work would be done in this room. Maybe the room would look regular to most people. But behind the secret panels and hidden doors . . .

Yes. She would do very important things behind this door. She heard footsteps coming up behind her.

"Liberty! I look forward to seeing this room," Miss Crum's voice said. "I went through some furniture and decorating catalogs with your mother."

"You did?" Liberty asked. Liberty's old room had been babyish. She still had the yellow comforter with baby ducks on them. She liked ducks, but puh-lease.

"Your family was able to pick any of the furniture from the White House collection," she said. "My choice was a white frilly princess look. With lots of ruffles. Wouldn't that be perfect?"

Okay, no. Liberty suddenly wasn't sure if she wanted to open her eyes. And she opened the door and peeked with one eye.

It was definitely not frilly or ruffled! Liberty grinned and opened both eyes.

Yesss!! Her room was her favorite kind of blue! There were bunk beds! There was a ladder to climb

up—and a slide to get down! There was a bulletin

board so she could stick up her pictures. There were

glow-in-the-dark stars attached to the ceiling.

"Franklin, look!" Liberty pointed.

There was a new light blue dog bed. There were

a ball, a rubber bone, and his favorite squeaky toy. Franklin ran over and jumped on his bed.

Liberty ran over to her bed! And then she saw her beanie dogs on the top bunk and on the shelves. Her beanie dogs! And new blue-and-white fluffy bed stuff! Liberty took out her cell phone and took pictures of her room.

"This was not what I was expecting," Miss Crum muttered. "Where are the lace curtains I suggested?"

"Liberty, what do you think?" Chief Usher Lee asked her.

"A+!" Liberty said. "That's the best!"

"Splendid," said Chief Usher Lee. "We will let you enjoy your room. Please let me know if you need anything."

Chief Usher Lee and Miss Crum stepped out of the room.

Liberty waited until the door was completely shut. And finally, Liberty was alone!

She pulled out some glasses from her bell bag. She wheeled the desk chair over to the line of dogs. "I've missed you!" Liberty picked up her stuffed animals one by one and gave them a special hug. Bella the bulldog. Julian the German shepherd. Bradley the black-and-white smiley dog.

And a new one! Someone had gotten her the rottweiler!! It had a red, white, and blue bow on it.

"I'll name her Alice," Liberty decided. The name came from Alice Roosevelt, one of President Theodore Roosevelt's daughters. Like Liberty, she also had been described as "spirited" and "high-energy." "I can't wait to sign her in to his virtual home. Just like we're moving into our new home!"

Liberty put the rottweiler on her desk.

"This is our new room," Liberty told her beanie dogs. "But it's also our new office."

She looked around to make sure nobody was listening.

"You are not only the First Stuffed Animals," she whispered. "You are my secret assistants. America is counting on us."

Liberty saluted the stuffed animals. She was sure they saluted back.

"But first," she said. "We go wild."

Liberty grabbed an armful of the beanies. She wheeled them in circles in the chair! She climbed up onto the top bunk and slid some beanie dogs down the slide. And she followed.

Woo-hoo!

Liberty climbed back up on her bed to see the view. This was the Best. Room. Ever! Seriously. She tipped backward with her head hanging down. It looked great upside down, too.

Liberty saw herself in her new mirror. She realized she was still wearing her coat and dress. Liberty had found out that what she wore on Inauguration Day was a Very Important Choice. She had read about it on the front page of the newspaper a couple weeks ago.

FIRST DAUGHTER WILL BE FASHION TRENDSETTER!
The World Is Watching
What Liberty Will Wear!

Hello? That was serious pressure! Liberty was not used to the world watching what she would wear!

Liberty had not been a fashion trendsetter in a sadly

long time. Not since preschool. That's when it was totally normal to wear a feather boa and superhero cape! And everyone knew Liberty had the best costumes.

Liberty had tried to keep the feather boa trend going in first grade. But everyone had laughed at her.

So when it was time to pick out her outfit for Inauguration Day, Liberty had an idea. If Liberty was going to set trends, she could wear a feather boa to Inauguration Day! Then kids all over America would want to wear feather boas!

And everyone who had laughed at her in first grade would be like, Oh, no! We never should have laughed at her! Liberty was *two years ahead* of fashion trends! And they'd all write her letters of *sorry* at the White House. Liberty would forgive them. But let that be a lesson to them!

It would have been a fashiontastic plan. Except

Liberty's mother said n-o to the feather boa. And y-e-s to the warm winter coat.

But now Liberty was in HER territory. She could be as fashiontastic as she wanted. She slid down the slide. Liberty whipped off her coat and flung it onto her desk chair.

"Franklin," Liberty said. "What should I wear?"

She looked over. Franklin was already asleep on his bed.

Yes, they were even going to sleep here! In fact she could put on her pajamas now if she wanted to. Because she lived here! She could run around the White House in her pj's! She could even wear her feather boa!

Liberty grinned. She opened her dresser drawers and there they were! Her favorite pj's with the stars on them! Liberty changed into them. She pulled on her favorite comfy slippers.

Liberty opened the door to her bedroom. She saw SAM standing in the hall.

"Um, I'm wearing my pajamas in the middle of Inauguration Day because . . ." Liberty didn't quite know how to explain this.

"No explanation needed," SAM said.

"Okay!" Liberty said. "I'm just going to look around the new place!"

Liberty ran. She slid down the floor. She tried a cartwheel but fell over. Too bad being the First Daughter didn't make her any better at cartwheels. She ran around and opened doors. There was a kitchen! There was her parents' room! It was already decorated in the old-fashioned furniture her mom had picked out from the White House collection. Some other presidents and their wives had used the same furniture before! Liberty smiled when she saw her parents' puffy white comforter from home. She'd snuggled up under that same comforter in her old house. Now she'd snuggle up in it in the White House!

Liberty ran on.

There was a room for she had no idea! There was a bathroom! There were the stairs!

Liberty raced down the stairs. That's right! In her pajamas! Liberty was running through the White House in her pajamas! This was like a dream come true!

Or was it a nightmare?

She heard SAM call her name. But it was too late.

Because she ran right into a whole room of grown-ups. And she was in her pajamas.

Chapter 5

LIBERTY WAS LUCKY. VERY, VERY LUCKY.

She could have gone through the other door. Then she'd be standing in the front of the room. But she was in the back. So all she saw were people's backs.

Big. Phew.

Liberty wondered what was going on. She wiggled into the crowd of people. Someone was speaking into a microphone. Everyone was listening.

"The president enjoyed the Inauguration Parade very much," the speaker said.

They were talking about her dad! Liberty wanted to stay. She could spy. Maybe she could tell her dad what they said. That would be something a Secret Assistant to the President would do!

"Any questions?" the speaker asked.

"What will be the first thing the president's family does when they settle in to the White House later?" someone asked.

Ooh! Good question! Liberty waited.

"I do not know the answer," the speaker said.

Wait! Liberty knew the answer! She had asked her parents that, too. They had let her choose!

"Oooh! Oooh!" Liberty waved her hand in the air. "Pick me! Pick me!"

Nobody saw her. Sometimes it was hard to be short. Liberty would have to just make herself heard.

"They're going to put on really loud music!" Liberty said in her very loud voice. "Then they're going to dance around to celebrate! And the president will dance his favorite dance, the bump!"

The room suddenly went silent. Everyone turned to look at her. To STARE at her.

Liberty felt a little awkward. Oh! Maybe they didn't know what the bump was?

"It's a funny dance?" Liberty said.

Liberty did a little bump move. Nobody moved. She leaned over to the lady near her and bumped her with her hip.

"It's the FIRST DAUGHTER!" someone said.

And then they all turned to her.

"Liberty, how do you like your new home?"

"Um," Liberty said, backing away. "I think I should be leaving now."

"Liberty, do you like your new bedroom? Liberty, why are you in pajamas? Is it your bedtime already?

Did you get in trouble and get sent to bed?"

The reporters started moving closer and closer. Some people held their microphones out.

And luckily SAM swooped down and guided her right out the door.

Chapter 6

AND THEN SAM GUIDED HER UP THE STAIRS into the residence, and down the hallway into her room.

"I'm thinking that wasn't such a good idea," Liberty said along the way.

"Run out of the residence and into a press conference?" SAM asked her. "And then hide in the crowd so I can't get to you without making a scene? No, that wasn't the best idea."

"Well, it could have been worse!" Liberty told him. "When Theodore Roosevelt was in the White House, his sons used to drop water balloons on people's heads at White House meetings!"

"That *would* have been worse," SAM agreed.

"Sorry, I was just trying to help," Liberty said. "The speaker guy didn't know the answer and I didn't want him to feel dumb!"

"I understand," SAM said. "I believe those reporters were not allowed cameras today, so we could be lucky."

Oh. Liberty hadn't even thought of that. Liberty's parents were careful about pictures. Liberty had learned that the hard way. Like when her dad first ran for office, Liberty had put bunny ears behind her father's head. Okay, they thought it was kind of funny when they saw it in the town newspaper.

"Once is a little funny," her mom had said. "Second time is not."

Okay, Liberty hadn't learned that lesson too well. Because then when they were taking her dad's picture

in a parade, she did her favorite goofy face, where she stuck her tongue out sideways and crossed her eyes.

"Liberty," her mother said, holding up the picture, "your father is smiling and waving. I am smiling and waving. We hope you enjoy yourself and want to smile and wave. But if you don't, please don't do bunny ears or goofy faces."

Liberty looked down at her pajamas. She wondered

if that included wearing pajamas and a boa and doing the bump.

"Maybe I should get changed out of my pajamas," Liberty said. But before she could do anything, she heard a voice.

"Liberty! Where are you?" a voice sang out.

Oh, no! Chief of Staff Miss Crum!

"Quick, toss on your coat," SAM said.

Okay! Great idea! Liberty opened her bedroom door and grabbed the coat she'd flung on her desk chair. She pulled off the boa and put her coat on over her pajamas. Then she kicked off the slippers and slid on tall black boots. Hopefully that would cover up her pj pants.

"Yoo-hoo!" Miss Crum stuck her head in the bedroom door.

Liberty buttoned up her last coat button. Whew! Just in time.

Chapter 7

H ELLO, MISS CRUM!" LIBERTY SAID.

"I have someone for you to meet," Miss Crum said.

And that's when Liberty noticed there were other people in the hallway. There was a woman with dark blond hair, a dark green dress, and dark green very high heels. And standing next to her was a boy who was about Liberty's age. He was kind of short and had dark blond hair with a lot of shiny goo on it. He was wearing a navy blue blazer with a light blue shirt and khaki pants.

"Liberty, I'd like to introduce you to Mrs. Piffle and her son, James," Miss Crum said.

"It's a pleasure to meet you, Liberty," Mrs. Piffle said.

"It's a pleasure to meet you, Liberty," her son James also said.

"Mrs. Piffle is the chief of protocol," Miss Crum said.

"It means my mother plans events when presidents and heads of countries from other countries visit," James said helpfully.

"The word *protocol* means 'manners,'" Miss Crum said.

Ah. Liberty got it. James was supposed to be a good influence on her. She'd had many good influences forced on her in her life. Like when her teacher moved her seat between Perfect Paige and the wall so Liberty would stop talking in class. Or when the teacher made Perfect Paige her field trip buddy even though all the other kids got to choose their own buddies. Except Max Mellon. His buddy was the teacher.

"Here is a welcome to the White House gift," James said, holding out a small white box.

"Thank you," Liberty said, opening it. It was a pretty pink picture frame.

"We thought you could put a picture of you and your parents from Inauguration Day in it," Mrs. Piffle said.

"I will!" Liberty said. "It's definitely a better present

than what President Andrew Jackson once got."

"What was that present?" Mrs. Piffle asked.

"A giant cheese," Liberty told him. "For real! It weighed more than one thousand pounds. And he left it sitting in the White House front hall for two years! And it stunk up the White House!"

Mrs. Piffle and Miss Crum both gasped.

"Two-year-old smelly cheese?" James said. "Did they eat it?"

"Don't worry," Liberty told him. "The cheese didn't mold or anything. A crowd of people actually came and ate it. Right in the White House."

"That made me kind of sick to my stomach," James said.

"Oh no, is your tummy feeling sick?" Mrs. Piffle asked him. "James does have a sensitive tummy."

"No, I just meant smelly cheese was gross," James said. "I didn't mean anything about my . . . tummy."

"Maybe your tummy is sick because it's been such an exciting day," his mother continued. "Remember how you threw up after Cousin Adam's birthday party?"

"Mother, that was *one* time, and I was four," James groaned. "And I ate five cupcakes."

"Oh yes, and that terrible blue ice cream that stained your lips blue for days," his mother said. "Maybe today is too much for you. Maybe you should go home now and take a nap."

Liberty decided to help him out.

"Maybe James could rest a little bit in my room right here," Liberty said. "And then when he feels better, he could show me around."

"What a nice offer!" Mrs. Piffle said. "And James would love to show you around. He fancies himself a bit of an expert on the downstairs."

"That sounds perfect," Miss Crum said.

"I'll be right downstairs planning the official visitor

welcome visit," Mrs. Piffle said. "James, here is your backpack of backup things."

"I know, Mother," James said. He took a green backpack from his mother as she leaned over and smoothed James's bangs down.

"We can welcome people to the White House!" Liberty said. "And make sure everyone feels welcome!"

"Now Liberty," Miss Crim said. "You don't need to do that. I made up a list of approved things you two may do."

She handed James a piece of cream-colored paper.

"Liberty, it was so nice to meet you," Mrs. Piffle said.

"You too! And now I'll show James my new room!" Liberty said. She grabbed his arm and dragged him inside.

Whew. Safe.

"We can hide here until they're gone," Liberty said. She held up her cell phone. "I'll have SAM tell me when the coast is clear. SAM is my Secret Service Man today."

"Okay," James said. "May I leave my backpack here? I don't really need it. My mother makes me bring an extra change of clothes. So embarrassing."

Liberty nodded, and James carefully placed the backpack on her chair.

"But first," James said, pulling a piece of paper out of his pocket, "Miss Crim made up this schedule of what I'm supposed to show you. Oh no, we're four minutes late to start. I'm supposed to have told you how the White House was built already."

James actually looked worried.

"So George Washington had the White House built, but John Adams was the first president to live here, in 1800," James said.

"Oh, don't worry. I learned all that when I did a report on the presidency for school," Liberty said. "And the cool stuff like how Garfield's son used to ride his bike down the Grand Staircase. He would ride down the stairs and then go flying through the hall!"

"We actually aren't allowed to do that," James said.

"Yeah, I guessed that," Liberty said. "But do you know any good stories like that? How about Abraham Lincoln's ghost living here!"

"There's not really a ghost," James said.

"I read that there is!" Liberty nodded. "He walks around in the Lincoln Bedroom! Isn't that down the hall?"

"Yes," James said, going over and opening the door. "It's right out there. But there's no such thing as ghosts."

And then they heard a weird moaning noise.

ARRRRoooo.

"It's Lincoln's ghost!" James yelled. "Run! No, wait, hide! No! Call the Secret Service!"

Chapter 8

JAMES!" LIBERTY SAID. "CHILL OUT! IT'S OKAY!"

"Maybe for you!" he yelled, jumping on to the bed and pulling a blanket over himself. "But I don't want to meet a ghost!"

"It's not Abraham Lincoln! It's Ben Franklin!" Liberty said.

"You can see him?" James yelled. "Can you see him? Is the ghost of Ben Franklin in the room?"

"It's not a ghost," Liberty said loudly. She went over and opened her bedroom door. "It's my dog!"

Franklin raced into the room. And he let out a howl.

"Aarrrrooo," Franklin howled. He ran over, and Liberty bent down to pat him.

"His name is Ben Franklin, but we just call him Franklin," Liberty said. "Franklin, say hi to James."

"It's okay," James said, still under the blanket. "I'm good."

"Oh. Got it. You're afraid of dogs," Liberty said.

"Not exactly afraid," James said. "Just sensitive to them."

He's afraid. That's what he really means, Liberty thought.

"Franklin won't bite or anything," Liberty said. "My old babysitter said he's better behaved than I am. But I'll put him on a leash for you."

James peeked out and waited until Franklin was leashed.

"Well, it could be worse," Liberty told him. "Calvin Coolidge had twelve dogs in the White House."

James shuddered.

"It could be way worse, even," Liberty said. "Herbert Hoover's son had pet alligators outside. Theodore Roosevelt's daughter even had a snake. She named it Emily Spinach!"

James looked kind of green, like spinach. Liberty decided to be kind and stop talking about animals for a little while.

"I'll keep Franklin over here," Liberty said, leading Franklin to the other side of the room.

"Thanks," James said.

There was a knock on the door, so Liberty went over and opened it.

"Just checking," SAM said. "I heard the dog."

"Franklin and James are just getting to know each other," Liberty said cheerfully. "We're cool."

"Ruffles is fine," SAM said into his ear thingy. Then he went back out of the door.

"Are you Ruffles?" James asked.

"Rrr," Liberty grumbled. "Yes. There are a bajillion words that start with R and I get stuck being 'Ruffles.' Ugh."

"Well, it could be worse. They could just call you DOPOTUS."

"Doh-what-us?" Liberty asked him.

"The president is also called POTUS," James said. "For President of the United States. First lady is FLOTUS. You'd be Daughter of POTUS. DOPOTUS."

DOPOTUS or Ruffles? Liberty sighed.

Liberty sat down on the bottom bed. Franklin came over and jumped up next to her.

"So Franklin would be what? DOG-POTUS?" Liberty asked.

"You're surrounded by DOG-POTUSES," James said, looking around. "You must have a million stuffed dogs."

"Thirty-two!" Liberty said, proudly. "I got a new dog today. The rottweiler."

James picked up a beagle.

"No, the brown and black one," Liberty said. She went over and picked it up. "This is a rottweiler. Rottweilers can be tough, so they need an extra good home."

She tossed the rottweiler to James.

"That should be your code name," James said. "Rottweiler. Starts with an R. And you're in a good home. The best one ever! The White House!"

Liberty thought about it. Rottweiler. She liked it. Maybe her "official" code name had to be Ruffles. But her Secret Assistant to the President code name could be Rottweiler! Excellent!

"Arrrooo!" Franklin howled.

James looked nervous.

"It's just Franklin! Not a ghost, remember?" Liberty

said. "Hey, let's go look for the ghost in Lincoln's bedroom!"

"Well," James said. "I have only heard about the ghost coming out at night. And I've kind of always wanted to see Lincoln's bedroom. He's my favorite president."

"You mean your second-favorite president," Liberty said. "Because President Porter is now your favorite because his pres-tastic daughter is going to take you to see the room!"

She waved to him to follow her. Franklin trotted after her.

"Uh, do you think SAM would come with us?" James asked her. "Just in case?"

Liberty, James, and SAM walked down the hall to the Lincoln Bedroom. SAM walked in first and said it was ghost-free. But Liberty waved hi just in case.

The room was very fancy, with a large bed in the middle. It had big curtains coming down from the sides. That was one big bed, she thought. It would be a perfect jumping-on-the-bed bed.

"Abraham Lincoln signed the Emancipation Proclamation in this room," James said. "It was in the middle of the Civil War. It was the first step to freeing all the slaves."

Whoa.

Liberty closed her eyes and felt the moment. When she opened them, she saw James was at a desk.

"And this is the Gettysburg Address," James said. "One of the most famous speeches in America. It's a copy signed by Abraham Lincoln himself."

James read the first few words.

"Four score and seven years ago," it read.

"A score is twenty years," James said. "So he was talking about eighty-seven years before that."

They were silent. Liberty walked over to the Lincoln bed. She pulled off her boots and climbed up on the bed. Liberty thought about that moment when Abraham Lincoln gave his famous speech. Maybe someday she would give a speech that would be famous too. Liberty wondered what her important speech would be about.

"Liberty?" James asked. "Can I ask you a question?"

"What I'd give an important speech about?" Liberty asked him.

"Uh, no," James said. "Are you wearing pajamas?"

"Oh." Liberty looked down at her swinging legs. "Yeah. I am."

And suddenly, Franklin barked. Then he poked his head under the bed and started sniffing.

"You know, dogs sometimes see ghosts," James said nervously. "Maybe your dog smells them."

"Um, actually I think he smells my boots," Liberty

said. She jumped off the bed and pulled her boots back on.

"Maybe we should go now," James said. "I'm spooked."

"And maybe I should remember to change out of my pajamas," Liberty said. Just to be on the safe side, she turned around and waved. "Bye, Mr. Lincoln! I'll be back."

They quickly left the Lincoln Bedroom.

"It's extra busy up here," SAM said. "The staff is unpacking your family's things here. Maybe we should head downstairs soon."

There were people moving boxes around the halls.

"Okay!" Liberty said. And then she said hi to people who were unpacking things.

"Hi, Liberty!" people answered. And some of them said, "Hi, James! Hi, Franklin!"

"Okay," James said, walking beside her. "Before we go downstairs I have to read you the rules."

James pulled out the paper Miss Crum had given him.

"Rule number one," he read. "Keep the First Daughter away from people who might talk to her."

"She said to keep me away from people?" Liberty said.

"And the china room. Because it's filled with breakable priceless china."

"I can't be around people or china?" Liberty asked. "Harsh! Where *can* we go?"

"Miss Crum says we can go to the Calligraphy Office," James read. "That's where they write out invitations with fancy pens."

"Bluh," Liberty said. "Miss Crum hasn't seen my handwriting. It's horrible. What else?"

James turned the paper over. It was blank.

"That's it?" Liberty asked. "All these awesome things in the White House, but Liberty Porter, First Daughter can't see them?"

And then Liberty had a brilliant idea.

Liberty Porter might not be able to see them. But Rottweiler could.

"I'm going undercover," Liberty said. She went over to her closet and opened it up.

"What are you talking about?" James asked.

"I'll wear a disguise!" Liberty said. "LIBERTY can't go around the White House because LIBERTY can't talk to people. But nobody will know it's me. We can go everywhere!"

"I'm not sure about this," James said.

Liberty opened her dresser drawer.

"I saved all my costumes," Liberty said, digging through. "I could wear my pop star outfit!"

She pulled out a wig and her glittery dark glasses.

"You would kind of stand out in that," James said.

True. Liberty pulled out a superhero cape and a vampire cape. Nope. A princess tiara and a witch hat. Nope.

"I know!" Liberty said. "I'll disguise myself as a boy! I can wear your clothes!"

"What? Then what will I wear?" James said. "Plus, my mother will get upset if my clothes are wrinkled or messy. That's why she makes me bring the extra outfit."

"Ding ding ding!" Liberty shouted and jumped up. "We have a winner! I'll wear your extra outfit!"

Liberty ran over to the backpack and opened it. She pulled out a navy blue jacket that looked exactly like the one James had. A light blue button-down shirt. And a pair of khaki pants.

"We'll be twin brothers!" Liberty said.

James left the bedroom and Liberty got ready. The

clothes didn't fit her perfectly, but they would do! James had on fussy shoes, but Liberty was done with being fussy. She put on sneakers so that she could move fast. Then, of course, there was her hair and face problem. Hmm. She found a pair of fake glasses and pulled the rubber nose off of them. And now she had to hide her long hair.

Hmm.

She found a couple of white baseball hats that said "I'm a Porter SupPorter" on them. Liberty scrunched and pushed her hair up underneath one of them.

She looked in the mirror. Awesome!

"Yo," Liberty said to Franklin. "Let's test out my disguise."

Secret Assistant to the President, code name Rottweiler, had some work to do. Mission: Exploring the White House.

Chapter 9

LIBERTY STEPPED OUT INTO THE HALLWAY.

"Yo, SAM," she said in a low voice.

"Sup, James?"

"Are you ready, Liberty?" SAM asked her.

"Rats, you knew it was me?" Liberty said.

"Well, I'm your Secret Service agent," SAM reminded her. "It's my job to know these things. Plus, who else would come out of your room?"

"Oh, yeah," Liberty said. "But isn't my disguise excellent? James, I brought you a Porter SupPorter baseball hat so we could match."

She placed the extra one on his head.

"Now don't blow my cover by calling me 'Liberty,'" Liberty said.

"Ruffles is leaving the residence," SAM said into his ear thing.

"Rottweiler!" Liberty whispered to James.

"Okay, let's go downstairs," James said. "This is the public part of the White House. More than a million people tour it every year."

Now *that* was going to be weird. In her old house, sure, she'd had her friends over after school. But more than one MILLION people? That was one seriously big playdate.

They got into one of the elevators. Liberty presssed the button and grinned.

She had elevators in her house. How cool was that?

The elevator opened.

Everything was so shiny and pretty. There was

beautiful art. There were flowers everywhere. There were pictures of the presidents and their wives hanging all over the walls.

Liberty felt like their eyes were watching her.

"So," SAM said. "Where do you want to go first?"

Liberty opened her mouth to answer. But first, her stomach answered the question for her.

Grumble. Grumble. Growl.

"Was that noise from your stomach?" James asked her. "It sounds like mine after I eat dairy."

Yes. It was. Liberty was suddenly very hungry, even though she had gone to the big Inauguration Lunch.

Here was the lunch menu:

Seafood stew

Pheasant served with sour cherry chutney

Molasses sweet potatoes

She had not eaten much at lunch. Liberty was not planning to be a picky person. But she had no idea what some of those things exactly were.

"I think I'm starving. Is there any food in this house?" Liberty asked them.

SAM laughed. Then he put back on his serious face.

"There are three kitchens!" James said. "There are some of the world's best chefs! They cook the finest meals! My mom told me you guys had pheasant for lunch. Yum!"

"Pheasant? Yum? Um," Liberty said. "Is that what I have to eat every day?"

"Don't worry," SAM said. "They can make anything you want."

Anything? Brownies for breakfast? Cake for lunch? Ice cream for dinner? And not just any ice cream, but four scoops of different flavors with hot fudge and sprinkles and extra whipped cream and—

"As long as it's fine with your parents, of course,"
SAM added.

Oh. That would be a normal meal with vegetables.

"I hear they make an excellent macaroni and cheese,"
SAM said.

"I love macaroni and cheese!" Liberty said. "It's on my top-five favorite food list:

5. Pancakes

4. Quesadillas with only cheese

3. Chicken nuggets

2. Mac and cheese

"And my number-one favorite food is dessert!" Liberty told them.

"Wait until you see what the pastry chefs make," James said. "And you've got to see the chocolate shop."

Liberty stopped in her tracks. Chocolate shop? CHOCOLATE SHOP?!!

"Nobody ever told me there was a chocolate shop!" Liberty said. "What are we waiting for?"

Liberty followed James down the steps and hall

that led to the pastry kitchen's chocolate shop.

"This is so awesome," Liberty said. "Except I don't have any money."

"It's not a shop where you buy things," James said. "They make chocolate. You get to eat it."

FREE CHOCOLATE SHOP!!

"Did you guys know there was a chocolate bar named after a First Daughter?" Liberty asked. "Baby Ruth was named after Grover Cleveland's daughter."

That would be awesome to have a candy bar named after you. But not called Baby Liberty. Maybe Choco-Liberty. Or the Liberty Crunchtastic. It would definitely have crunch in it. But no coconut.

And suddenly Liberty smelled something. It was the best smell Liberty had ever smelled. There were men and women in white coats and tall chefs hats. They were all very, very busy. But they stopped when Liberty walked in and looked up.

"Sorry," she said. "I didn't mean to interrupt. Keep chocolate-ing."

"Come in, come in," one of the chefs said. "Welcome, boys."

And then Liberty remembered.

"Oh!" she said. "I'm Liberty Porter under here! I'm in disguise so I can walk around the White House!"

And hopefully get chocolate.

The chefs were all, like, we would have never guessed! What a great disguise!

"And this is James," Liberty said. "He's really a boy and not a girl."

"Isn't that obvious?" James asked her.

"Just making sure they know," Liberty told him.

"Would you like to see what we're working on?" the chef said.

The chef showed them a long table that had bunches of flowers on them.

"This is the flower shop, too?" Liberty asked.

"No, that's nearby. These flowers are all made of chocolate," the chef said. "Try one."

"No way!" Liberty said. They totally looked like real flowers. She took a pink petal and licked it. Then she ate it.

"Yum!" Liberty said. Then she looked and saw little animals marching on a tray.

"Those aren't candy, are they?"

"Yes," the chef said. "It's a tradition to make either elephants or donkeys on Inauguration Day. They represent either the Republicans or the Democrats."

Liberty peeked at them close up. They looked so real and teeny!

"For a state dinner for India, we made chocolate white tigers," the chef said. "For Kenya, we made giraffes. I wonder if I should create little candy dogs some time."

Liberty turned around to see Franklin waiting down the hall with another Secret Service agent. Franklin stood up on his hind legs like he was begging.

"Franklin, they're going to make little candy yous!" Liberty said. That would be so cute!

"We need some official testers for the butter cookies." A chef brought over a tray with giant cookies. They all had pictures of the White House on them done in white icing.

"Me! Me!" Liberty and James raised their hands.

Liberty and James took their official taste test.

"This is made of awesome! A+ Awesomely Perfect!" Liberty announced. Everyone cheered!

"Would you like to take a few more to test?" the chef asked. He handed Liberty and James extra cookies in a baggie.

"This house gets better every minute!" Liberty said happily as they left the wonderful heaven that was the White House chocolate shop.

Chapter 10

T HE ROOM NEXT DOOR IS THE BOWLING alley," said James.

"You are so on," Liberty said. "I accept your bowling challenge!"

"Well, I wasn't challenging you," James said. "I was just—"

"I will crush you!" Liberty crowed. "I will take you down!"

"Okay," James said.

"James, you're supposed to say you're going to beat me!" Liberty said. "Show some spunk."

"Well, I'm not really good at bowling," James said.

"Neither am I!" Liberty said. "So repeat after me: You're gonna lose with a capital L!"

"You are going to lose with a capital L?" James said. He didn't sound very convincing.

"We'll work on it." Liberty sighed. She followed James into the bowling alley. It was a real bowling lane. It had the score-keeping thing and everything! Which was good, because Liberty was not particularly excellent at adding correctly.

"I don't think it's set up to actually bowl right now," SAM said.

Liberty noticed that the lane was slick and shiny.

"Is it set up for a superslide?" Liberty asked him.

SAM nodded. Liberty took her sneakers off and got in position. She ran as fast as she could and . . .

Wooosh!

Liberty slid down the perfectly slick lane! She

stopped before she got to the little gate blocking the pins, of course. Franklin ran alongside her, barking happily.

"James," she said. "Come on!"

"I don't know," James said. "I'm not a bowling ball."

"Take off your shoes!" Liberty insisted.

James took off his shoes. And slid down the lane. And smiled.

"Not bad," Liberty said. "What else is down here?"

"The movie theater," James said. They walked out of the bowling alley and down the hall to the theater.

Liberty couldn't believe she'd have her own movie theater. And it had a popcorn machine. It had fifty chairs in it. The screen was huge.

"In the White House movie theater you get movies before they even come out in the theaters," James said. "Sometimes real-live movie stars will come to watch their movies with the president."

Pres-tacular!

"I call front row!" Liberty called out. She ran to the front. There were feet-cushion things that you could put your feet up on. So, she put her feet up on them. Comfy.

Wait a minute. Liberty didn't have to sit. Liberty lived here. She cleared her throat and prepared to "star" in her own movie.

"The movie is about to begin. Please take a seat!" Liberty announced. SAM and James sat in the chairs. Franklin sat on the floor.

"Presenting *Liberty Porter: The Movie*!" Liberty announced. She went over and dimmed the lights.

"Is this a scary movie?" James asked. "I'm not allowed to watch scary movies."

"No," Liberty said. "It's an action-adventure movie."

She stood in front of the screen.

"Liberty Porter *seems* like a normal girl," Liberty said dramatically. "But she's really a crime-fighting super-hero!"

Liberty flew around the room. Well, ran around. Franklin chased her, barking. The audience went wild! Well, James and SAM clapped for them, anyway.

"With her sidekick Franklin, she saves the world!" Liberty announced.

Suddenly Franklin started barking.

"What is it, sidekick Franklin?" Liberty said. "Is there an evil villain about to attack innocent people?"

Franklin whimpered. Then he whined. Then he started sniffing around.

"Uh-oh," Liberty said. "You'll have to wait for *Liberty Porter: The Sequel.* Franklin has to *go*."

Chapter 11

LIBERTY, JAMES, AND FRANKLIN QUICKLY followed SAM out of the theater, up the stairs, and to a hallway on the main floor.

"There's a security exit right here," SAM said. "Hand me his leash. I'll take him out. Please stay put."

"Thanks, SAM!" Liberty said.

James and Liberty could see SAM through the glass window. It looked like Franklin was being a good boy.

And then Liberty saw a group of kids walking down the hall.

"Happy Inauguration Day!" she said in a deep

voice that she hoped sounded like a guy's. They all walked on by.

"See, nobody knew it was me!" Liberty said. "I'm just some boy. This is awesome!"

Then a woman in a long gold and dark green dress and a man in a suit walked by them.

"I think it is this way," the woman said.

"I believe we passed it," the man said. "Or did we?"

"Watch this!" Liberty whispered to James.

"Hello!" she said in her guy voice. "Are you lost? Can I help you find your way?"

"Thank you, son," the man said. "We're looking for the library. We're a bit late."

"We can show you the way," Liberty said.

"James," she whispered. "Where's the library?"

"Through that room," he said. "But we can't leave here, remember?"

"We will assist you," Liberty said loudly to the

people. Yes! Finally, a job for the Secret Assistant to the President. The White House would continue to be known for its excellent treatment of guests.

"This way, please!" Liberty said.

The two people followed her out. James followed too, looking nervous.

"Are you enjoying your visit to the White House?" Liberty asked.

"We are," the woman said. "It is very special."

"Yes," Liberty said. "The new president has said he will make it even more special with . . ."

With what?

"Porter Butter Cookies!" Liberty said. "Please have a White House special memory cookie." She handed them each a cookie.

"I will bring it back to my son. He has a sweet tooth." The woman smiled.

"Did you know that George Washington had a

dog named Sweet Lips?" Liberty asked them.

"I did not know that," the woman said.

"Here's the library," James said. They walked into a room with bookshelves all the way up to the ceiling. "There are 2,700 books here."

Liberty's mom was going to love this place. Her code name was Reader. At least *her* official code name fit her.

"Enjoy your visit!" Liberty said to the man and woman.

"Thank you for showing us," the woman said. "And for the cookies."

Liberty and James walked out of the library.

"There are books about all the presidents and their families," James said. "Hey! Maybe someone will write a book about you, Liberty!"

"Awesome!" Liberty said. Now *that* would be too cool. Liberty felt pretty good about things.

"So were you kidding about George Washington's

dog's name?" James said. "Did you make that up?"

"Nope!" Liberty said. "It was Sweet Lips! That's a true historical fact!"

"How about the Porter Butter Cookies?" James asked her.

"Well, I made that part up," Liberty said. "But it's genius! Look how happy they were when I gave them cookies. Everyone should be happy at the White House."

Just then a grown-up followed by a group of kids walked past them.

"People! This is not a place for fun and games!" the grown-up was saying. "No laughing! Keep your hands to yourselves!"

The group of frowning kids followed him into the next room.

"That must be the tour of new kids," James whispered. "Their parents work for your father now."

Liberty watched the kids. They didn't look too happy. Liberty remembered her last field trip at her old school. They had gone to the zoo. One person had puked on the bus ride there. Max Mellon had eaten the animal food pellets instead of feeding them to the llamas. That made Perfect Paige puke.

It was very memorable. Liberty wanted to make this field trip memorable for these kids, too.

"Come on," Liberty whispered. "Let's just go in for a second."

"We have to go back to SAM," James whispered.

"We're just going right there," Liberty said. "Just one second."

She went into a small living room with green walls.

"The Green Room is one of three state parlors on the first floor . . . ," the tour leader was saying.

"Usually a Secret Service agent gives the tour," James whispered. "But I don't know who that guy is."

"And people, notice the curtains in watered silk, in a vertical and moiré pattern."

Liberty had no clue what that meant. And she lived here.

Liberty saw a kid yawn. Then she saw two kids poking each other. And then the group started to leave. Wait! The tour leader hadn't even told them anything interesting about the Green Room!

"He didn't even say anything about the painting of Benjamin Franklin or the one by painter Jacob Lawrence," James whispered.

Even James noticed this tour was lame. The kids all shuffled as a group to the next room. Liberty followed.

"Children," the leader said, "this is the Red Room."

The Red Room! It had deep red walls and red chairs. Liberty saw a picture of Dolley Madison on the wall.

Liberty had learned all about how Dolley Madison had lived in the White House during the War of 1812.

And then the British came and burned the White House down! But Dolley was a hero for saving a famous picture of George Washington that still hung in the White House today.

Liberty closed her eyes and pictured Dolley Madison racing out just before the British arrived! When she opened her eyes she noticed other people had closed their eyes too. But they looked more like they were falling asleep.

Chapter 12

THE ROOM IS TWENTY-EIGHT BY TWENTY-five feet," the leader went on and on and on.

Blah, blah, blah. The leader was sucking the life out of these rooms! These were some of the most amazing rooms in the White House! Okay, maybe not as cool as the movie theater. Or the bowling alley. Or the chocolate shop. Okay, nothing was as cool as the chocolate shop.

Liberty couldn't take this anymore. She raised her hand.

"Is there a question?" the leader said.

"Yes," Liberty said, in her guy voice. "Did you know that President Teddy Roosevelt's kids used the Red Room as a playroom and walked all over this place on stilts?"

Everyone turned to look at her.

"And did you know the teddy bear was named after Teddy Roosevelt?" Liberty asked.

"Questions may be asked after the tour," the leader said. "Now let's look at the wallpaper."

"I didn't know that about the teddy bear," an older girl wearing a HELLO MY NAME IS Quinn name tag read.

"I'm not sure your leader is telling you about the really cool parts of this house," Liberty whispered.

"Dude, no kidding," the boy next to her said in a low voice. "Our parents are all excited to work here. I'm wondering why."

"That's Mario's father giving the tour," Quinn whispered to Liberty. "He was supposed to just be the parent chaperone. But he said he wanted to give the tour instead of the woman who works here, Miss Yee."

Liberty needed to assist these poor people. They were in the White House! On Inauguration Day! And they were being BORed!

"There are a lot of exciting things going on right now," Liberty told them. "Did you know the president and his family are moving in upstairs right now?"

"That's cool," a girl said.

"I bet that Liberty Porter is really stuck-up," said another girl tagged HELLO MY NAME IS Nicole. "She's upstairs with her servants getting all spoiled. I bet she never comes downstairs to where normal people are."

Well, hello. Liberty was here! She was *not* stuck-up! She was normal!

"Children! May I please have your attention!" the

leader who was somebody's father said loudly. "We will divide into two groups. Everyone in Group A please follow me to examine details on the wallpaper."

Hello My Name Is **Nicole** went with Group A.

Liberty would show them she was normal and not stuck-up.

"Group B, please follow Miss Yee," Mario's father said. "Miss Yee will take you to the Blue Room to examine its wallpaper. Choose a line leader and be sure everyone walks single file."

Liberty followed Hello My Name Is **Quinn** over to Group B.

"I guess we have to choose a line leader." Miss Yee smiled. "How about the boy in the hat?"

And Miss Yee pointed to Liberty. Liberty saw everyone turn to look at her. And then Liberty saw someone else looking at her.

It was SAM. And he was walking her way. And he didn't look too happy. Oops.

"Yo! Sure, I'll be line leader!" Liberty said in her guy voice. She quickly went and stood right next to Miss Yee.

Liberty started walking really quickly. James followed behind her, and ten kids after him. SAM followed, also very quickly.

"Hello, Miss Yee," Liberty heard SAM say. "I'll be joining you for a little bit."

"Of course," Miss Yee said. "We're going to visit the Blue Room."

Liberty passed the Blue Room and kept walking.

"You just passed the Blue Room," James whispered to her.

Liberty continued as SAM caught up with her and walked alongside her.

"Hi!" Liberty whispered to him. "Where's Franklin?"

"I left him with another agent," SAM said in a low voice. "My fellow agents were reporting to me that you were moving from room to room. As I was taking your dog to the bathroom."

"Um," Liberty said. "But you knew where I was, right?"

"I always will know where you are," SAM said. "But it will be helpful if you stay where you are supposed to be. And, by the way, where are we going?"

Liberty pretended she didn't hear that. She headed all the way up toward the residence and started up the stairs.

"Do you have permission to do this?" James asked.

"Their parents all work for my dad," Liberty said. "They're kids just like you! Right, SAM?"

"Well, they are approved to visit the White House,"

SAM agreed. Liberty heard him mumble something into his earpiece. "Gbrrrr. Dbrrrrr."

"Hm," Miss Yee said. "This isn't on our tour."

"I know!" Liberty squealed.

She took off her glasses. She pulled off her hat and shook her hair out.

"You're Liberty Porter!" everyone gasped.

Chapter 13

T HAT'S ME!" LIBERTY SAID. "ALSO WHITE
House tour guide, taking you to my new
bedroom!"

The kids stood in the room with their jaws dropped.
Miss Yee stood in the room with her jaw dropped.

"Come on. I want to show people my new room so
bad," Liberty said. "Please?"

Everyone was like, Duh! Of course they were coming!
They all crowded in her room.

"We're backstage at the White House!" one girl
said. "Can we ask questions?"

"If you have a question, please raise your hand," Miss Yee said.

Liberty knew people had a lot of questions for her. When her father was running for president, reporters had asked her some pretty boring ones.

- Are you proud of your father?

  (Yes, of course.)
- Are you excited to live in the

  White House? (Yes, of course.)
- Will you miss your old home?

  (Yes, of course. Except living on the

  same street as Max Mellon.)

Some reporters asked her questions that made her parents say, "Okay, enough of that!" Like:

- Are you going to have a baby sister

or brother when you're in the White House? (**What?!!!**)

"How much is your allowance?" asked a girl whose name tag read HELLO MY NAME IS Yasmin.

"Two dollars a week." Liberty sighed.

"Yeesh, I get more than that," said a boy whose tag read HELLO MY NAME IS Cheese Fries.

Miss Yee gasped.

"It's okay," Liberty said. "Any other questions, *Cheese Fries*?"

Miss Yee peered at the boy's name tag and looked surprised. "Is your name really Cheese Fries?" she asked.

"No, it's Jack," the boy said. "But I like Cheese Fries. So do you get every single game system and video game that comes out? Like all the companies just send you everything for free?"

Liberty thought about what her parents said over and over: *We want Liberty to grow up living as normal a life as possible.*

She guessed that meant she wouldn't have every game system for free.

"No," Liberty said. "I'll just get normal stuff."

"When you met the Bonus Brothers, did you freak out?" Quinn asked.

Okay, she had to admit that had been SO not normal!!!!

"I was so nervous! And when we got our picture taken, I thought I was going to throw up," Liberty said.

"You did not," Cheese Fries scoffed.

"No, I totally did," Liberty said. "Look at the picture!"

She pointed to a picture on her bulletin board.

"Oh," Cheese Fries said. "You *do* look like you're going to throw up."

"Are you going to go on their TV show?" a girl asked.

"No," Liberty said. "My parents definitely said I can't go on any good TV shows. Just boring news ones with them."

That was kind of a bummer. Liberty had hoped it would be like: Special Guest Star: Liberty Porter! Or they would make a cartoon sponge that looked like her and she would get to talk in a funny voice. But nope.

"You're lucky you can make a mess in your room and people will clean it up for you," said a boy wearing HELLO MY NAME IS Mario tag.

"Nope," Liberty says. "I still have to clean my room. And do my chores. But people are going to cook for me!"

"Do you get room service?" a girl asked.

"She can call the White House kitchen," James suddenly spoke up.

"I can?" Liberty said. Oh, yeah! She could!

"SAM, can you ask the kitchen to send up cookies for everyone?" Liberty asked.

Everyone cheered.

"I wish I could live in the White House." Quinn sighed.

"Maybe you will after me!" Liberty shrugged. "Or maybe you'll be president!"

"That bed is sweet," Mario said.

"Want to slide on it?" Liberty asked.

Mario scrambled up the ladder. And slid down the bed. And then everyone wanted to try! People climbed up and slid down.

"I have more of these than you do." Cheese Fries held up a stuffed animal.

He reminded Liberty of a certain Max Mellon. She

picked up a stuffed pug and aimed. *Bam!* Score!

"Hey!" the boy said. "The First Daughter just hit

me in the head with a pug!"

He threw the pug back.

"It's on!" Liberty yelled, grinning.

And then everyone grabbed a beanie dog and started throwing them around. Beanie dogs were flying everywhere!

And then there was a knock on the door. The cookies had arrived! Everyone grabbed a cookie, even Miss Yee!

"Best field trip ever!!!" someone whooped.

And then:

"WHAT IN THE WORLD?"

Liberty looked up. Just in time to see a beanie black labrador hit Miss Crum's nose.

Oops.

Chapter 14

AND THIS IS THE OVAL OFFICE," JAMES WHISpered. "It's where the president works."

Miss Yee's group had rejoined the rest of their tour group—on the public floor. Miss Crum had called Liberty's parents. They were now waiting to meet her dad in the Oval Office.

"And see that desk?" Liberty whispered back. "There's the secret door in the desk where John F. Kennedy Jr. used to hide out in when he was really little."

Miss Crum gave them a *You are in trouble, so why are you talking?* look.

Liberty supposed maybe it was a good time to take a break in their tour.

Miss Crum had not been happy with the kids in Liberty's room. Or the stuffed animals all over. Or the cookies they'd been eating in there. She had expressed that quite loudly as Liberty was getting changed in her room. Liberty decided it was best to change out of her disguise and into what she thought Miss Crum would think was a more "appropriate" outfit. Miss Crum was still not happy. Not happy at all.

Even Franklin knew it. He was lying with his head on his paws on the carpet.

The carpet had the Seal of the President on it. A giant eagle with a banner over its head that said *E pluribus unum*. Liberty's father had told her it was a special saying in Latin that meant "out of many, one."

"The United States was first made up of many colonies," her father had told her. "And America is made up of many people of many backgrounds. We all come together to form one great nation. Out of many, one."

Liberty had looked forward to seeing it. But not exactly while waiting to get in trouble.

Suddenly, extra Secret Service agents came into the room. And there were her parents!

"Hi, Mom! Hi, Dad!" Liberty said. "Mom, Dad, this is my friend, James Piffle. He's been giving me a tour of the White House."

"Good afternoon, Mr. President," James said. "Good afternoon, Mrs. Porter."

They shook hands.

"Thank you for giving Liberty a tour of the White House," her father said.

"Ahem," Miss Crum said. "I'd like to discuss this tour they went on."

She looked over at James. He looked worried. Liberty knew this was all her fault. She would take the blame.

"Excuse me," Liberty said. "I think Franklin has to go."

Everyone looked at Franklin. He was sitting there.

"The dog seems fine," Miss Crum said.

"I just don't want him messing up the special carpet," Liberty said. "James should probably take Franklin out."

"Me?!" James said. He gave a worried glance at the dog.

Liberty gave him a look that said, *Go! Get out of here! Escape!*

"Perhaps Sam could help them," Liberty's father said.

SAM, James, and Franklin left the room. James walked as far away from Franklin as he could.

"Mr. President," Miss Crum said. "Mrs. Porter. I think we need to take care of something. We have very important events this evening. And Liberty has acted a bit inappropriately today."

Inappropriate was one of Liberty's least favorite words.

"Liberty invited children from a tour group into her bedroom. And they caused bedlam!"

Um.

"Liberty interrupted a press conference," Miss Crum said. "Then she did the bump with a reporter from a major television news program!"

Er.

"Liberty also wore pajamas and dressed in boy's clothing outside the residence. Liberty could become a major embarrassment to the White House!" Miss Crum said. "She could become an embarrassment to the United States of America!"

Liberty got the sick feeling in her stomach. Liberty suddenly felt very ashamed. She was going to be an embarrassment to the country!

She was the worst First Daughter ever.

Chapter 15

EVERYONE WAS LOOKING AT LIBERTY.

"I didn't mean to be an embarrassment to anybody," Liberty said softly.

"Why did you interrupt a press conference?" her father asked.

"The speaker didn't know the answer. So I wanted to be helpful," Liberty said.

"Why did you bring children into your bedroom?" her mother asked.

"I wanted to make everyone feel welcome in the White House," Liberty said. "I thought they'd want to see my new room. Plus, okay. The dad who was leading the tour was boring everyone. He didn't say any of the interesting things about the White House!"

"Why were you dressed as a boy?" her father asked.

"I was undercover as a boy," Liberty said. "I wanted to be a normal person and see the White House."

Liberty's father suddenly walked over to the desk. He sat down in the tall chair. There were two flags on either side of him. He had a very serious face. Liberty's father looked very much like a president of the United States.

Maybe now that he was the president, he couldn't be so much her father. She took a deep breath. She prepared to hear her official punishment.

"Of course, in any home we live in, Liberty must follow the house rules," her father said. "Including the White House."

Miss Crum nodded and smiled.

"That said, it sounds like Liberty *is* trying to help make the White House a home," her father said. "In her own unique way. And for the right reasons."

Miss Crum stopped smiling.

"Liberty's mother and I chose the name Liberty for a reason." The president turned to look right at Miss Crum. "Liberty means the right to act, believe, or express oneself in a manner of one's own choosing."

Liberty's father winked at her. And Liberty's father gave her a smile.

"We encourage Liberty to act, believe, and express herself as a First Daughter in her own original and creative way," her father said.

"We like our original and creative First Daughter," her mother said. "We want her to stay that way."

Liberty suddenly felt very happy. Very, very happy.

Miss Crum looked very uncomfortable. Very, very uncomfortable.

Suddenly the door opened. A Secret Service agent came in.

"Excuse us, Mr. President." He went over and said something in a low voice to Liberty's father.

"Send them in," her father said.

SAM came in holding Franklin on a leash. He was followed by James and Chief Usher Lee.

Franklin whined.

"Excuse me, Mr. President," Chief Usher Lee said. "It was brought to my attention there might be a misunderstanding. There have been no house rules broken. The staff has already been charmed and delighted by Liberty."

"Please don't punish her!" James suddenly burst out. "She just wanted people to feel welcome in the White House!"

"James, do not worry. It's been all cleared up," the president said. "However, I'm sure Liberty appreciates your support."

James let out a big *whew*.

"Miss Crum," her father said. "I believe I am greeting some visitors shortly. Can you please check on them to see if they feel welcome in the White House? And please, do not worry about Liberty. That's my job."

Miss Crum opened her mouth. But all that came out was a little noise like "uh." And she left the room.

Liberty's mom and dad gave her a big huge family hug.

Chapter 16

LIBERTY AND HER PARENTS WERE GOING to greet the official guests.

They were Very Important People from a Small, Faraway Country.

James was coming with them. His mother's job as chief of protocol was to help visitors from other countries.

It would be Liberty's first official guest greeting!

"They're from a country that has been having a difficult relationship with the United States," James said. "I heard my mom talking about it."

Okay. This was a lot of pressure. Liberty smoothed her favorite party dress, which had a secret pocket the just right size for her new cell phone. Nobody had told her she had to change her outfit. But she had run upstairs and put on a dress. She was going to be on Best. Official. Behavior. She took out a sparkly silver fancy purse. She also stuck in a Porter Butter Cookie just in case they served pheasant snacks or something.

They went into the Blue Room.

James was there with his mother.

"Hello, Liberty." James's mother smiled at her. "Thank you for sharing your day with James."

"Oh, I still have his backpack," Liberty said. "Um, I kind of borrowed his extra outfit. But Chief Usher Lee said he would get it all clean and unwrinkly again for you!"

"Oh." James's mother looked confused.

"So my dad said James was a ginormous help today!"

Liberty quickly added. "He's an awesome tour guide. My father said he would want to hire James when he gets older."

"Then we both could work for the White House," James said to his mother.

His mother beamed. "James! I'm so delighted! You're such a good boy!"

James stayed with his mother as she gushed over him, while Liberty followed her parents over to the guests.

Liberty's parents introduced her to a woman, a man, and a teenager boy.

Hey! The grown-ups were the people who had gotten lost earlier. Liberty started to remind them, but realized she'd met them when she was wearing her disguise. And had sneaked away from SAM. So maybe it was better not to say anything.

"We hope you enjoyed your visit to the White House," Liberty's mother said.

"Thank you," the Official Visitor Woman said.

The visitors weren't smiling. They all sort of stood there. Awkward!

Just then Liberty noticed one of the boy's shirt pockets was moving. And then a little tiny animal stuck its head out. It looked like a tiny white mouse, sort of. It had big eyes, big ears, and a stripe on its head.

Suddenly Official Visitor Woman looked at her son and gasped.

"Oh, no!" she scolded. "President Porter, I apologize for my son. He brought one of his pets without permission."

The boy looked guilty and tried to push the little animal back into the pocket.

"Excuse me, what is that?" Liberty asked. "I never saw one of those before."

"It's a sugar glider," the boy said. "It's called a

sugar glider because it loves sweet foods. It's a small

marsupial. The female has a pouch like a kangaroo."

"Is it friendly?" Liberty asked. "May I pet it?"

"Yes. Ours are friendly," the boy said. "We raise many sugar gliders."

"I appreciate your daughter being kind about this situation," the Official Visitor Man said to Liberty's father. "I did not intend to bring this animal into your White House."

"Our Liberty loves all animals," Liberty's father said.

Liberty reached out to pet the sugar glider. It was cutetastic!

"Presidents in the White House have had lots of unusual pets," Liberty told them. "There were bear cubs and tiger cubs."

"Bears and tigers?" her father asked. "I did not know this."

"Yup. And there was a raccoon named Rebecca and a badger named Josiah. And lion cubs, alligators, and a pygmy hippopotamus."

"Fascinating! We love animals too," Official Visitor Woman said to Liberty. Everybody smiled.

Suddenly the sugar glider took flight. It had wings! It jumped out of the boy's pocket. And jump-flew onto the curtains!

"Oh, no!" everyone yelled.

"I'll catch it!" the son said. He ran over to the curtain. But the sugar glider jumped over his head! And onto an old table! And ran into the next room.

And that's when Liberty heard a bark. Oh, no! Franklin must have smelled the sugar glider!

Everyone rushed through the door and into the diplomats' room. Franklin was barking and chasing the jumping sugar glider! There went the dog chasing! Everyone was grabbing at the sugar glider! Or the dog!

"Oh, no!" James's mother gasped. "This is an international disaster!"

And suddenly James grabbed Franklin's collar. "I got

the dog! I got the dog!" he yelled. "Sit, Franklin!"

And Franklin sat.

Now for the sugar glider! Wait! Sugar! That gave Liberty an idea. She remembered the cookie. She unsnapped her purse and held it open.

The sugar glider hung from the curtain. It looked around and sniffed. Then it jump-flew over to Liberty's shoulder.

"Eeps!" Liberty said. Then the sugar glider dove into her purse for the cookie.

"Got it!" Liberty said. And closed her purse.

"Bravo!" the Official Visitor Man shouted.

Everyone cheered. The son took the sugar glider out of the purse and put it back into his pocket.

"How did you do that?" Official Visitor Woman asked Liberty.

"It was the cookie," Liberty said. She held up the rest of it.

"Isn't that a Porter Butter Cookie?" Official Visitor Man asked. "Hmm. You look oddly familiar. Do you have a brother?"

"Um," Liberty said.

"Liberty was in disguise as a boy today so she could help people," James said. "She wanted everyone to feel welcome in the White House. It was the only way."

"So *you* are the kind young person who gave us a Porter Butter Cookie and helped us when we were lost!" Official Visitor Man said.

Liberty nodded.

"Ah! You should be proud of your First Daughter." Official Visitor Woman turned to Liberty's parents. "She gave us a wonderful welcome to America's White House."

Liberty grinned. Her parents grinned. Everyone grinned.

Franklin made his happy dog bark. Aroooo!

Suddenly the sugar glider poked out of the boy's pocket again! And it jump-flew onto the desk. Oh, no! Not again!

But this time it jumped onto Franklin's back! And it stuck to Franklin's collar. And Franklin turned around. And gave the sugar glider a lick!

"They're friends!" Liberty said.

"Dogs and sugar gliders can be friends," the son agreed. The son picked up the sugar glider and held it up to Franklin. Franklin sniffed. The sugar glider made a noise like *chirp!*

Everyone laughed.

"What a wonderful day for all of us," Official Visitor Woman. "And we would like to present an official gift from our country to yours. Liberty, please accept the sugar glider."

Her son nodded and held out the sugar glider to her.

"What?" Liberty said.

"We wish you to have it as a pet. In fact, they should live with a friend. So we will give you two," said Official Visitor Man.

Liberty looked at her parents.

"We can give you a cage and special food," the son said.

"Well, we'll have to follow the rules for foreign gifts," the president said.

James's mother came over and whispered something to him.

Liberty crossed her fingers as much as she could and still hold the sugar glider. She closed her eyes and made a wish. Please could she keep the sugar glider!

And then suddenly the sugar glider jump-flew out

of Liberty's crossed fingers. And onto the person walking in. Miss Crum!

Oh, no! Liberty was doomed.

"Ack!" Miss Crum squealed. "What is this on me?"

"It's a sugar glider," Official Visitor Woman said. "It is a gift from our country to your wonderful First Daughter. A thank-you for her generous welcome to the White House."

"Another pet?" Miss Crum looked at the sugar glider. She looked at Liberty.

"It could be worse," Liberty's father said. "It could have been an alligator or a pygmy hippopotamus. We can be the first First Family with a pet sugar glider!"

He winked at Liberty.

"That's pretty historical!" Liberty agreed.

"Well," Miss Crum said weakly. "Pets do teach

responsibility to children. And the press does love to report on White House pets. Erm. Liberty, would you please remove your new pet?"

Liberty grinned and ran over.

"Welcome to the White House, sugar glider!" Liberty said, picking it up. Liberty thought its sweet little face was smiling.

Suddenly a woman entered the room. And she was followed by some kids. It was Miss Yee!

"Oh, sorry," she said. "We thought this was on the tour."

"Hey, there's Liberty Porter!" someone yelled. It was Cheese Fries!

"Hi!" Liberty waved back.

"Liberty Porter rocks!" Cheese Fries yelled.

"Liberty Porter rocks!" The whole group started clapping and cheering.

The president and first lady were smiling at her. The

Official Visitors, James, and SAM were smiling at her. Miss Crum was . . . well, at least she was not frowning at her.

Maybe Liberty wasn't going to be a *perfect* First Daughter. But she had a feeling she was going to be a pretty good one.

Chapter 17

PRESENTING THE PRESIDENT AND THE first lady!" the announcer announced. "Our honored guests at the first-ever Liberty Ball!"

The night of a new president's inauguration, there are lots of fancy balls around Washington. The president and first lady get all dressed up and dance the night away.

Okay, so this one wasn't exactly a real ball. Liberty had made up her own Porter family party. It was taking place in Liberty's new home, in the hallway near her bedroom. The guests were Liberty and her parents. And the beanie dogs that were lined up along the walls.

And the announcer was Liberty, talking into her battery-operated pop star microphone.

Liberty had put on a velvet jacket over her party dress. It had a pocket that was a perfect fit for her sugar glider. Now the sugar glider could be part of the festivities too!

Liberty started singing the "Hail to the Chief" song.

"Doo doo do DO! Do do dee do do do dooo!"

Franklin sang along, "Arrrooo! Arroooo!"

Her father and mother stepped out into the hallway from the kitchen. Her father twirled her mother around as Liberty clapped for them. Her father looked all fancy in a tuxedo. Her mom looked beautiful in a deep blue gown.

Liberty ran over and turned on her MP3 player.

And then her father started doing the bump with her mom! And then he turned around and bumped Liberty! And then her parents took her hands and all three of them started dancing around! Past the Lincoln Bedroom! Past the Queen's Bedroom!

"Prestastic!" Liberty said.

And then Liberty looked up and saw SAM and James.

"Welcome to the Liberty Ball!" Liberty said to them. She looked down the hall. Her parents were now twirling around. "First, dancing! Then, movies and snacks!"

Liberty's parents had let her pick out some movies to watch in the White House movie theater. Liberty had invited the kids from the tour whose parents worked for her dad too. Even Cheese Fries.

"Guess what?" Liberty said to James. "We're going to the chocolate shop to make our own sundaes! The flavors are chocolate, cookie dough, and blue supermoon!"

"I'm not allowed to have blue ice cream," James said. "It stains my lips blue."

"You are if your mother says you can!" Liberty said. "I even asked her!"

"I *never* get to have blue ice cream!" James said happily.

"We'll be celebrating. But first, we have some secret official business," Liberty said. Liberty pulled James off to the side of the hallway. She gave SAM the planned signal.

SAM crossed his arms and looked official.

"James Piffle," Liberty said in a serious voice, "you have proved yourself an official patriotical person today. You assisted the Secret Assistant to the President today. And you showed bravery with dogs."

SAM turned to James. "Upon official request of the First Daughter," SAM said, "the *secret* Secret Service is giving you a secret code name."

"Really?" James said. "My own code name?"

"Unofficial. But still excellent," SAM said. "Your code name is . . . Whippet."

"A whippet is a dog that's shy and sensitive at first,"

Liberty told him, "but gets braver and is really loyal to its friends."

"Whippet?" James said. "I like it."

Franklin barked.

"Franklin, I didn't forget about you," Liberty said. "You are my new Secret Canine Rover Assistant to the President. SCRAP. Your official code name is SCRAPS!"

Franklin liked that. Definitely.

Liberty's parents were twirling their way back down the hall toward everyone.

"Announcing guest James Piffle! And Secret Agent Man SAM," Liberty said loudly.

"James! Sam!" Liberty's parents waltzed over to them. "Welcome! Please join us in a dance!"

"Thank you, but I'm a horrible dancer," said James.

"You may be be a bad dancer but you *are* a good slider!" Liberty shouted. "Come see the best slide ever!"

It was better than the bowling alley lane. Better than the East Room shiny floor. There was a ramp to a room called the solarium. And you could slide all the way down—on your butt!

SAM took Liberty's velvet jacket and sugar glider for her.

Liberty took a running start and sliiiiiiiiiid!

James took a running start and sliiiiiiiiiid!!

They slid three times. Then Liberty's felt a buzz in her pocket. Her cell phone! She read a text from her father.

Plz join me 4 a father-daughter dance.

POTUS

Liberty and James went back up to see them. And Liberty ran almost right into Chief Usher Lee! And, oh. Miss Crum. Miss Crum was dressed in a long, fancy red ballgown.

"I hear there's an exciting ball going on up here." Chief Usher Lee smiled.

"Yes, well, it's almost time for your parents to leave for the balls," Miss Crum said.

"Attention everyone," Liberty yelled. "Presenting Miss Crum! And Chief Usher Lee! Guests of the Liberty Ball!"

"Thank you, but I wasn't planning to stay," Miss Crum said.

"You can't miss the first ever Liberty Ball," Liberty said. "It's a very exclusive invitation."

Liberty grabbed the startled Miss Crum's hand to keep her from leaving.

"Just in time for our last dance," Liberty's father said when he saw them. "It's the president and First

Daughter Father-Daughter Dance."

Liberty's father bowed to her. She curtsied. He took her hands. She put her feet on his shoes. And he started to dance.

Liberty's mother clapped as Liberty's father twirled her down the hall. They twirled past her bedroom.

"I think the Liberty Ball will be my favorite tonight," her father said. "I've danced with my two favorite people in the world."

"Yay!" Liberty said as they twirled past the Queen's Bedroom and the Lincoln Bedroom.

"You have represented the kids of America well today," her father said.

"Do you think that Miss Crum thinks so too?" Liberty asked.

"Her job is to watch over my business and not yours," her father said. "However, I firmly believe

anyone who gets to spend time with you will grow to appreciate you."

They twirled back down the hallway just as the sugar glider peeked its head out of Liberty's pocket.

"So have you thought of a name for your new pet?" her father asked.

"I can't think of the perfect one," Liberty said. "Any ideas?"

"I always thought George Washington had an interesting name for his pet dog," her father said.

"I know!" Liberty said. "SWEET LIPS!"

However, Liberty said it a little too loudly. And just as they were dancing by Miss Crum.

"Excuse me?" Miss Crum asked. "Did you call me Sweet Lips?"

"Um," Liberty said. She looked at her father. He was trying hard not to laugh.

"I did try a new lipstick," Miss Crum said.

"And it looks really sweet!" Liberty said. "And that's why I said that! Because I thought your new secret code name could be Sweet Lips! I thought you should have a code name, too! I didn't want you to feel left out!"

"Why thank you, Ruffles," Miss Crum said. "That's very thoughtful of you."

Liberty's father twirled her off down the hall. And then they totally started cracking up.

"That was rather brilliant," her father said. "See, I knew you would win over even Miss Crum."

"You mean 'Sweet Lips,'" Liberty said. And cracked up again.

"I guess we have to think up a new name for the sugar glider," her father said. "Sweet Lips is taken."

"I know!" Liberty said. "Maybe we could ask the kids of America to vote. Can we ask on a website or something?"

"Sounds like a great idea," her father agreed. "We'll put it up on our website."

Just then a new song came on from down the hall. It was a fast and dancey song.

"I think it's been a successful Inauguration Day," Liberty's father said. "I couldn't have done it without you, First Daughter."

Really? He couldn't have done it without her?

They danced back up the hallway Her mother was dancing with Chief Usher Lee! James was sort of dancing next to Franklin! And SAM was dancing with Miss Crum! And everyone—EVERYONE—was smiling.

"Prestastic!" said Liberty. "And . . . First Daughter Fantabulous!"

Many thanks to my:

CHIEF USHERS: Mark McVeigh and Ellen Krieger, editors who ushered this book so awesomely

CHIEF *and* STAFF: Jon Anderson, Bethany Buck, Karin Paprocki, Alyson Heller, Bess Braswell, Venessa Williams, and Paige Pooler

SECRET SERVICE (LITERARY) AGENTS: Mel Berger, Lauren Whitney, Nicole David, Julie Colbert, and everyone at the William Morris Agency

FIRST HUSBAND: David DeVillers

FIRST DAUGHTER AND SON: Quinn and Jack DeVillers

FIRST DOG: Bradley Scruff DeVillers

LIBERTY PORTER, FIRST SUPPORTERS: Jennifer Roy, Robin Rozines, Amy Rozines, Melissa Wiechmann, Lisa Yee, Mitali Perkins, Tricia Wolfe, and Sabrina Bryan

DATE DUE

NOV 0 4 2010	
SEP 1 5 2014	

BRODART, CO.